To parents

*All children like a story at bedtime
and it is important that parents should share
their enjoyment.*

*Every child is different.
This collection of stories is intended to please
the varying tastes and abilities of boys
and girls between the ages of three and six.*

Any time is storytime!

Eileen Colwell

Contents

Acknowledgments:
Eileen Colwell (compiler), and the publishers, would like to thank the following for permission to include:
"The little red jersey" from *Stories to tell in the Nursery school* by Lilian McCrea (1950). Reprinted by permission of Oxford University Press; "Tadpoles" by permission of the Society of Authors as the literary representative of the estate of Rose Fyleman; "When I was One" by A A Milne from *Now we are six*, by permission of Methuen Children's Books, also from *Now we are six* by A A Milne © 1927 by E P Dutton and Co. Inc. Renewal 1955 by A A Milne. Reprinted by permission of the publisher, E P Dutton Inc., New York and also by permission of the Canadian publishers, McClelland and Stewart Ltd, Toronto; "Clever Polly" reprinted by permission of Faber and Faber Ltd, from *Clever Polly and the stupid wolf* by Catherine Storr; "Hob Nob" by Ruth Ainsworth, with her kind permission; "Marching in our wellingtons" from *Speech Rhymes* by Clive Sansom, by permission of Adam and Charles Black (Publishers) Ltd; "Sea" by Leonard Clark from *Stranger than Unicorns* and "Down the stream" by Spike Milligan from *Silly Verse for Kids* both by permission of Dennis Dobson, publishers; "The lost kitten" and "The bus that wouldn't go" both from *Stories to tell to the Nursery* by Margaret Law, by kind permission of Susan Jack; "White fields" from *Collected Poems* by James Stephens, by permission of Mrs Iris Wise and Macmillan, London and Basingstoke, also © 1915 by Macmillan Publishing Co. Inc., New York, renewed 1943 by James Stephens; "The little wooden soldier" from *The Pirate Ship and other stories* by Ruth Ainsworth, by permission of William Heinemann Ltd (Publishers); "The Little Car is looked after" from *The Little Car* by Leila Berg, by permission of Methuen Children's Books; "The hot potato" from *Some Time Stories* by Donald Bisset, by permission of the author and Methuen Children's Books; "Mrs Peck Pigeon" from *Silver, sand and snow* by Eleanor Farjeon, by permission of Michael Joseph Ltd; "The little hare and the tiger" from *More stories and how to tell them* by Elizabeth Clark, by permission of Hodder and Stoughton Ltd; "Alfred and the fierce, fiery fox" by Helen Cresswell with her kind permission; "What a surprise!" from *Tales of Joe and Timothy (Read aloud books)* by Dorothy Edwards, by permission of Methuen Children's Books; "The baker's cat" from *A Necklace of Raindrops* by Joan Aiken, by permission of Jonathan Cape; "Rabbits go riding" and "Elephant Big and Elephant Little", both by Anita Hewett, with her kind permission; "A bargain for the Brambles" © 1982 Ursula Moray Williams; "The cupboard" from *Collected Rhymes and Verses* by Walter de la Mare, by permission of the Literary Trustees of Walter de la Mare and the Society of Authors as their representative; "If you find a little feather" from *Something Special*, © 1958 by Beatrice Schenk de Regniers. Reprinted by permission of Harcourt Brace Jovanovich Inc., New York.

First Edition

Bedtime Stories

compiled *by* EILEEN COLWELL
illustrated by JENNIE SCHOFIELD,
MARGARET GOLD and DAVID ANSTEY

Ladybird Books Loughborough

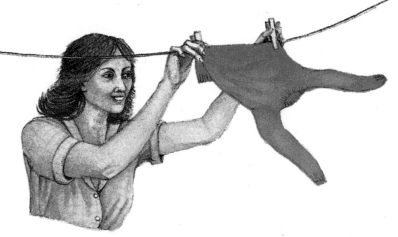

The little red jersey

Whish! Whee! sang the wind, and the trees tossed their branches and shook off their leaves. 'It's snowing leaves,' laughed Timothy.

'Yes,' said Mummy, 'it is a windy day today. I think I'll wash your little red jersey; it will dry in no time at all.'

'Oh, yes,' said Timothy, 'and then I can wear it at my party tomorrow.'

So Mummy washed the little red jersey, rub-a-dub-dub, scrub-a-dub-dub, in lovely warm soapy water. Then she took it out into the garden and pegged it on the clothes line. 'There,' she said, 'you'll soon be dry now, Little Red Jersey.' And then Mummy went back into the house and shut the door.

And the little red jersey out on the line began to dance and wave about. 'This is fun,' he said.

'Ha, ha!' laughed the wind. 'I want to have some fun too. Come on, I'll take you for a ride!'

'Oh, no,' cried the little red jersey.

'Oh, yes,' laughed the wind, and he tugged and tugged with all his might till down came the little red jersey, right off the line!

'Oh, dear,' he cried. 'Whatever's happening to me?' But before he had time to think, there he was sailing along in the sky, over the roof-tops and over the hedges, over the gardens and over the fields. On and on he sailed, on and on, until he came to a great brown oak tree and there he stopped, caught in the middle of its twisted branches.

'Where do you think you're going, Little Red Jersey?' asked the oak tree.

'I don't know,' cried the little red jersey. 'The wind blew me off the line and I must go home because Timothy wants to wear me tomorrow.'

'Well, you'll have to stay here now, until somebody helps you down,' said the oak tree, 'because my arms are old and stiff, and I can't move them.'

'All right,' said the little red jersey. 'I'll have to watch for somebody to come and help me.'

Presently a brown cow came strolling along. 'Moo-oo-oo. Hello, Little Red Jersey,' she said. 'What are you doing up there?'

'Oh, please help me down, Mrs Cow,' cried the little red jersey. 'I must go home because Timothy wants to wear me tomorrow.'

'I would if I could,' said the brown cow, 'but I'm not tall enough to reach you.' And off she strolled.

Presently a black-and-white horse came trotting along. 'Neigh. Hello, Little Red Jersey,' he said. 'What are you doing up there?'

'Oh, please help me down, Mr Horse,' cried the little red jersey. 'I must go home because Timothy wants to wear me tomorrow.'

'I would if I could,' said the black-and-white horse, 'but I'm not tall enough to reach you.' And off he trotted.

Presently a frisky lamb came skipping along. 'Baa-aa-aa. Hello, Little Red Jersey,' he said. 'What are you doing up there?'

'Oh, please help me down, Baa-lamb,' cried the little red jersey. 'I must go home because Timothy wants to wear me tomorrow.'

'I would if I could,' said the little frisky lamb, 'but I'm not tall enough to reach you.' And off he skipped.

'Oh, dear,' cried the little red jersey. 'Nobody can help me. I'll have to stay here for ever and ever.'

'Wait a minute,' said the oak tree. 'Look who's coming now!' And the little red jersey looked and saw a tiny grey squirrel scampering up the tree!

'Hello, Little Red Jersey, what are you doing up here? Are you looking for acorns, like me?'

'Oh, no,' cried the little red jersey, 'I'm just waiting for someone to help me down because I want to go home. Will you help me?'

3

'No,' said the wind, 'because I haven't any hands. But I'll leave you here on the doorstep and Timothy's Mummy will find you.'

And when Mummy opened the door, there was the little red jersey on the doorstep. 'Good gracious!' she said, lifting him up. 'Have you blown off the line? Why, you're all black; I'll have to wash you all over again!' And she took the little red jersey into the house and rub-a-dub-dub, scrub-a-dub-dub, she washed him again in lovely warm soapy water. 'There!' she said. 'I'll dry you by the fire this time, so that you won't blow away again.' And she spread the little red jersey on a clothes-horse in front of the warm glowing fire. And oh, how happy he was!

'Now I'll be ready for Timothy to wear at his party tomorrow,' he said. And he stretched himself out to dry his very best.

Lilian McCrea

'Of course I will,' said the squirrel and he pushed the little red jersey off the tree! And before he had time to say 'thank you', the wind came along and caught the little red jersey again.

'Oh, Mr Wind, please take me home. Timothy wants to wear me tomorrow,' he cried.

'All right,' laughed the wind. 'I was only having a little fun. I'll have you home in exactly one minute.'

And the little red jersey went sailing home in the sky, over the fields and over the gardens, over the hedges and over the roof-tops, until he came to his very own garden. 'Can you peg me back on the line, Mr Wind?' he asked. 'I want to get dry.'

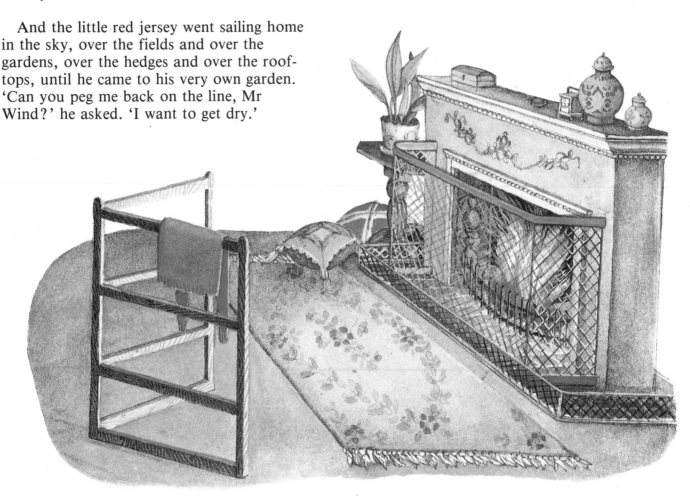

Tadpoles

Ten little tadpoles playing in a pool,
'Come,' said the water-rat, 'Come along to school,
Come and say your tables, sitting in a row';
And all the little tadpoles said, 'No, no, no!'

Ten little tadpoles swimming in and out,
Racing and diving and turning round about,
'Come,' said their mother, 'dinner-time, I guess';
And all the little tadpoles cried, 'Yes, yes, yes!'

Rose Fyleman

When I was One

When I was One,
I had just begun.

When I was Two,
I was nearly new.

When I was Three,
I was hardly me.

When I was Four,
I was not much more.

When I was Five,
I was just alive.

But now I am Six, I'm as clever as clever.
So I think I'll be six now for ever and ever.

A A Milne

5

Clever Polly

One day Polly was alone downstairs. Camilla was using the Hoover upstairs, so when the front door bell rang, Polly went to open the door. There was a great black wolf! He put his foot inside the door and said:

'Now I'm going to eat you up.'

'Oh no,' said Polly, 'I don't want to be eaten up.'

'Oh, yes,' said the wolf, 'I'm going to eat you. But first tell me, what is that delicious smell?'

'Come down to the kitchen,' said Polly, 'and I will show you.'

She led the wolf down to the kitchen. There on the table was a delicious-looking pie.

'Have a slice?' asked Polly.

The wolf's mouth watered, and he said, 'Yes, please!' Polly cut him a big piece. When he had eaten it, the wolf asked for another, and then for another.

'Now,' said Polly, after the third helping, 'what about me?'

'Sorry,' said the wolf, 'I'm too full of pie. I'll come back another day to deal with you.'

A week later Polly was alone again, and again the bell rang. Polly ran to open the door. There was the wolf again.

'This time I'm really going to eat you up, Polly,' said the wolf.

'All right,' said Polly, 'but first, just smell.'

The wolf took a long breath. 'Delicious!' he said. 'What is it?'

'Come down and see,' said Polly.

In the kitchen was a large chocolate cake.

'Have a slice?' asked Polly.

'Yes,' said the wolf, greedily. He ate six big slices.

'Now, what about me?' said Polly.

'Sorry,' said the wolf, 'I just haven't got room. I'll come back.' He slunk out of the back door.

A week later the door bell rang again. Polly opened the door, and there was the wolf.

'Now this time you shan't escape me!' he snarled. 'Get ready to be eaten up now!'

'Just smell all round first,' said Polly, gently.

'Marvellous!' admitted the wolf. 'What is it?'

'Toffee,' said Polly calmly. 'But come on, eat me up.'

'Couldn't I have a tiny bit of toffee first?' asked the wolf. 'It's my favourite food.'

'Come down and see,' said Polly.

The wolf followed her downstairs. The toffee bubbled and sizzled on the stove. 'I must have a taste,' said the wolf.

'It's hot,' said Polly.

The wolf took the spoon out of the saucepan and put it in his mouth:

OW! HOWL! OW!

It was so hot it burnt his skin off his mouth and tongue and he couldn't spit it out, it was too sticky. In terror, the wolf ran out of the house and NEVER CAME BACK.

Catherine Storr

Hob Nob

Once upon a time there was a red engine called Hob Nob. He had his name painted in black letters on the side.

Behind the engine was the tender. Behind the tender a string of trucks – one, two, three, four, five, six trucks. At the end of the trucks was the guard's van.

'Puff-puff-puff!' said Hob Nob, as he went along the lines. 'Puff-puff-puff!'

One day Hob Nob met a lamb.

'M-aaa!' said the lamb. 'Will you give me a ride to the fair?'

'Yes, I will,' said Hob Nob. 'Jump in.'

So the lamb jumped into the first truck.

Then Hob Nob met a dog.

'Bow-wow!' said the dog. 'Will you give me a ride to the fair?'

'Yes, I will,' said Hob Nob. 'Jump in.'

So the dog jumped into the second truck.

Then Hob Nob met a cat.

'Me-ow!' said the cat. 'Will you give me a ride to the fair?'

'Yes, I will,' said Hob Nob. 'Jump in.'

So the cat jumped into the third truck.

Then Hob Nob met a duck.

'Quack-quack!' said the duck. 'Will you give me a ride to the fair?'

'Yes, I will,' said Hob Nob. 'Jump in.'

So the duck jumped into the fourth truck.

Then Hob Nob met a hen.

'Cluck-cluck!' said the hen. 'Will you give me a ride to the fair?'

'Yes, I will,' said Hob Nob. 'Jump in.'

So the hen jumped into the fifth truck.

Then Hob Nob met a turkey.

'Gobble-gobble!' said the turkey. 'Will you give me a ride to the fair?'

'Yes, I will,' said Hob Nob. 'Jump in.'

So the turkey jumped into the sixth truck.

On they went – 'Puff-puff-puff-puff!' – with the lamb in the first truck, the dog in the second truck, the cat in the third truck, the duck in the fourth truck, the hen in the fifth truck and the turkey in the sixth truck.

Soon they came to a tunnel, and the tunnel was dark and sooty black.

'M-aaa!' said the lamb. 'I don't like the black tunnel. I don't like its black mouth. I think it will eat me up.'

'Bow-wow! Me-ow! Quack-quack! Cluck-cluck! Gobble-gobble!' said the dog, the cat, the duck, the hen and the turkey, all together. 'We don't like the black tunnel either!'

'Never mind,' said Hob Nob. 'I will blow my whistle when we go into the dark. I will make up my fire now, and send out sparks all the way through the tunnel. Then you won't be frightened.'

So he blew his whistle, 'Toot! Toot! Toot!' and he sent out lots of bright sparks: red ones and yellow ones. Then no one minded the black tunnel.

When Hob Nob got to the fair, he put on his brakes, and the tender and all the six trucks stopped. The lamb got out of the first truck, the dog got out of the second truck, the cat got out of the third truck, the duck out of the fourth, the hen out of the fifth and the turkey out of the sixth truck.

The lamb went on the roundabouts.

The dog went on the swings.

The cat went on the big dipper.

The duck had some candy floss.

The hen had an iced lolly.

The turkey had a drink of ginger pop.

Hob Nob had a nice nap in the sunshine, which was what he liked best.

So they ALL had fun.

Ruth Ainsworth

The turnip

Once upon a time there was an old man, an old woman, their grandchild, Susie, a black-and-white cat and a little mouse. They all lived together in a little house. Behind the house was a garden where the old man grew cabbages, carrots, onions and turnips for their dinner.

One day the old man went into the garden and dug a little hole and dropped into it one TURNIP seed. 'Grow well, little seed!' said the old man and he went indoors again.

The turnip seed grew. The sun shone, the rain fell, the wind blew and the seed became a small green shoot and, after a long time, a GREAT BIG TURNIP.

'Good!' said the old man. 'Wife, boil some water in the biggest saucepan we have, for we'll have turnip soup for supper. Now I'll go and pull up the turnip. I won't be long.'

Off he went into the garden, took hold of the green turnip top and pulled. The turnip would not come up. The old man pulled and pulled with all his strength, but it was no use.

So he called to his wife to help him. She came just as she was, in her apron. She put her arms round the old man's middle and the old man and the old woman pulled together. They pulled and pulled and pulled – but the turnip would *not* come up.

Then the old woman called to her grandchild, Susie, to come and help. And Susie came out just as she was, in her pinny, and put her arms round her granny's middle, and then the old man and the old woman and Susie pulled and pulled and pulled – but the turnip would *not* come up.

Then Susie called to the black-and-white cat to come and help. And the black-and-white cat stopped watching the mousehole and came running out, her tail in the air. Then the black-and-white cat put its paws round Susie's middle and the old man and the old woman and Susie and the black-and-white cat pulled and pulled and pulled – but the turnip would *not* come up.

Then the black-and-white cat called to the mouse to come and help. But the mouse said, 'Oh, no! You will eat me up!'

'No, I won't, not today!' promised the black-and-white cat, so the little mouse came running. It put its paws round the black-and-white cat's middle and the old man and the old woman and Susie and the black-and-white cat and the mouse pulled and pulled and pulled – and POP!!
THE GREAT BIG TURNIP CAME UP!

It came up so suddenly that the old man fell on to the old woman and the old woman fell on to Susie and Susie fell on to the black-and-white cat and the black-and-white cat fell on top of the little mouse (and nearly flattened it). And on top of them all was the TURNIP.

Then the old man and the old woman and Susie and the black-and-white cat and the little mouse carried the great big turnip into the house and made it into turnip soup. There was enough soup for everyone and the little mouse's wife and his seven children had some too. It was delicious soup!

Traditional

Marching in our wellingtons

Marching in our wellingtons,
  Tramp, tramp, tramp,
Marching in our wellingtons,
  We won't get damp.

Splashing through the puddles
  In the rain, rain, rain –
Splashing through the puddles,
  And splashing home again!

Clive Sansom

Sea

Over the hill
first sight of the sea
lying sunlit and still
just waiting for me.

I race from the land
in the clear morning light
to rock pool and sand,
shells whiter than white.

Birds ride the sky,
the wispy clouds there
soft floating, and I
am walking on air.

11

Leonard Clark

Simon's unlucky day

Mr Poppleton and Simon lived with Mrs Poppleton in a little white house far out in the country. Simon was a very clever dog. He had a long nose which smelt everything, long floppy ears which heard everything and dark keen eyes which saw everything. His legs were very short but they took him everywhere he wanted to go. When he was happy, he held up his long pointed tail in the air.

Simon understood everything that Mr Poppleton said to him and Mr Poppleton understood exactly what Simon wanted to say when he barked 'Wuff, wuff!', so they got on very well together.

One hot day in June, Mrs Poppleton decided that it was just the right kind of day for a picnic.

She packed up some food, Mr Poppleton piled cushions into the boat so that she would be comfortable, and Simon hurried to jump into the boat for fear he might be left behind. He always sat in the bow of the boat so that he could catch all the delicious smells that the wind blew over the water.

They were going to picnic on a small island in the bay. The boat moved slowly across the water with Simon at the front, pointing his nose into the breeze. Mrs Poppleton sat back comfortably and Mr Poppleton rowed and looked out for water birds.

Suddenly a fish leapt out of the water right under Simon's nose. 'Wuff!' he barked

and sprang forward to catch it. Splash! He fell into the water! He was most surprised to find himself there and Mr and Mrs Poppleton laughed and laughed. They knew Simon could swim very well and would reach dry land before they did.

That's just what he did. By the time the boat reached the shore, Simon was shaking himself and dashing about, barking.

'Off you go!' said Mr Poppleton. 'Have a run and get yourself dry, you silly dog!'

Away ran Simon to see what he could find that was interesting. He saw a squirrel run up a tree, but what was the good of chasing a squirrel – *he* couldn't climb. Following an interesting scent, he found a mole hill. 'Here's a good place to dig,' he thought. He scraped with his paws so hard that the soil flew in all directions.

But he couldn't find the mole for he had escaped through his back door.

Away went Simon again. 'Squawk!' A brightly coloured pheasant started up at his feet. Simon jumped quickly and snapped at its tail feathers, but he was too late, it got away. 'I wish I could find something I *could* catch!' thought Simon. 'Things shouldn't run so fast, it isn't fair.'

He smelt the ground with his long nose and picked up the fresh scent of a rabbit. As he ran, he caught sight of its white scut, disappearing down a hole in the warren. He sniffed eagerly, then began to dig frantically, pushing his nose further and further into the sandy hole. To his dismay when he tried to pull it out again, he couldn't. He was stuck! How would he ever get out? 'Wuff, wuff!' he said, in a muffled kind of way. 'Help, help!' But there was no one to hear.

On the other side of the little island, Mr Poppleton was wondering where Simon had got to. 'Simon!' he called, clapping his hands. 'Come here!' But there was no answering bark. Mr Poppleton knew that Simon was an obedient dog and always came when he was called. Could something have happened to him? He set out to look for Simon, calling and whistling as he went. No answer.

Suddenly he caught a faint 'Wuff!' It seemed to come from underneath the ground. Could it possibly be Simon? Then he saw something long and thin waving frantically at the mouth of a rabbit hole. It was Simon's tail!

'Whatever are you doing, pup!' exclaimed Mr Poppleton. He took hold of Simon's long body and pulled and pulled. Out came Simon like a cork from a bottle and sneezed and sneezed to shake the sand out of his nose. He was covered with sand and soil, one ear was inside out and he was panting with the heat and thirst. Mr Poppleton brushed him down as well as he could, but it was a very miserable dog that crept up to Mrs Poppleton to be patted and comforted.

Soon Mr and Mrs Poppleton and Simon were back in the boat again. This time Simon would have been glad to fall into the water, he was so hot and uncomfortable.

At home again, Mr Poppleton said firmly, 'A bath for you, Simon!' and fetched the dog-bath into the kitchen. Simon hid under the dresser but it was no good. He was soaped and rinsed and rubbed dry until his coat was as smooth as velvet. Mrs Poppleton gave him the food he liked best of all and he drank and drank from his bowl marked 'DOG'. He was so tired that he flopped into his basket without being told to. Mr Poppleton watched him burrow under his rug, until only his long nose was pointing out of the folds, and then he said, 'Goodnight, Simon.'

But Simon didn't even say 'Wuff, wuff!', for he was dreaming already of chasing squirrels and rabbits. The long summer day was over.

Vera Colwell

The lost kitten

One day Mummy said, 'I've brought you a surprise,' and she put a basket on the table in front of Susan. Inside it was a little black kitten for her very own.

'His name is Sooty,' said Mummy. 'You must be kind and play gently with him because he is so small. He has just left his mummy to come to you, so he's feeling a little sad.'

Susan stroked him softly. She gave him a saucer with a little warm milk in it, and made a paper ball for him to run after. She played with him all morning till dinner was ready, in case he should feel lonely. Then she ran off to wash her hands.

When she came back she looked for Sooty but she couldn't find him.

'Sooty, Sooty, where are you?' she called, but he didn't come. So Mummy and she had to look for him. They looked under the table and under the chairs and behind the curtains, but they couldn't find him. They went into the bedrooms and looked under the beds and on top of them too, but he was not there. They looked in the cupboards and in the wardrobes and in all the dark corners, calling, 'Puss, Puss, Puss,' but he wasn't to be seen.

Poor Susan was very upset. 'He's such a very small pussy,' she said. 'He might not know his way and be lost for ever.'

But Mummy said, 'He must be somewhere in the house. We just haven't looked in the right place.' So they started to look again. They looked, and looked, and looked, and at *last* they found him. I wonder if you could guess where? – Curled up fast asleep inside of one of Mummy's big furry boots.

How Susan laughed when she saw him. 'No wonder we took such a long time to find him,' she said.

Margaret Law

14

White fields

In the winter time we go
Walking in the fields of snow;

Where there is no grass at all;
Where the top of every wall,

Every fence and every tree
Is as white as white can be.

Pointing out the way we came –
Every one of them the same –

All across the fields there be
Prints in silver filigree;

And our mothers always know,
By the footprints in the snow,

Where it is the children go.

James Stephens

15

The little
wooden soldier

There was once a little wooden soldier with a little wooden gun. He wanted to guard somebody, and keep them safe. But he lived in the back of a dark cupboard, and no one ever took him out.

So he made up his mind to go into the world and see what it was like. He started off one morning, tramp, tramp, tramp in his black boots. Soon he came to a cat fast asleep in the sun.

'I'll guard the cat,' said the little wooden soldier, and he marched up and down, taking care of the cat.

Then the cat woke up and stretched.

'What are you doing?' she asked. 'Marching up and down and waking me up?'

'I was guarding you,' said the little wooden soldier.

'Well, I don't need guarding,' said the cat. 'Go away!' And she showed her sharp, pointed teeth and her curved claws.

So the little wooden soldier went on his way, tramp, tramp, tramp in his black boots. Soon he came to some baby chicks, pecking in the farmyard.

'I'll guard these baby chicks,' said the little wooden soldier, and he marched around and around them, taking care of them.

Then the mother hen appeared, clucking loudly and fluffing out her feathers. 'Cluck! Cluck! Cluck! What are you doing to my baby chicks?'

'I was guarding them,' said the little wooden soldier.

'Well, they don't need to be guarded,' said the hen. 'I can take care of them myself,' and she snapped her beak in his face.

So the little wooden soldier went on his way, tramp, tramp, tramp in his black boots. Soon he came to some baby ducklings. They were near the edge of a pond.

'I'll guard these ducklings,' said the little wooden soldier. 'I'll see that they don't fall into the pond,' and he marched up and down, and was very busy keeping the ducklings safe.

Then the mother duck swam to the shore, quacking loudly.

'What are you doing?' she asked. 'Marching up and down so my children can't get into the water where they belong?'

'I was guarding them,' said the little wooden soldier.

'Well, they don't need guarding, and they don't need to be kept away from the water. Come to me, children. Heads up! Paddle with your feet! That's the way!' And the ducklings swam along behind their mother, as happy as could be.

So the little wooden soldier went on his way, tramp, tramp, tramp in his black boots. Soon he came to a snail, hiding under a leaf. Now a snail is a very, very timid person indeed, but the soldier thought he had better *ask* if she wanted to be guarded.

'I should like to be guarded very much,' said the snail. 'I never feel safe for a minute. I'm afraid of the thrush who is waiting to eat me. First he will crack my shell on a stone, and then he will gobble me up.'

'Don't be afraid any more,' said the little wooden soldier. 'I'll watch out for the thrush and keep him away. You go where you please. I will take care of you.'

So he followed the snail along the edge of the lawn, and across a flower bed, and under the rhubarb leaves. When the thrush came near, the little wooden soldier fired his gun. 'Bang! Bang! Bang!' and the thrush flew away.

The little wooden soldier became well known in the garden. He guarded young caterpillars, and baby spiders, and families of beetles.

'Whatever did we do before we had a soldier of our own to take care of us?' said all the garden folk.

Ruth Ainsworth

17

The Little Car
is looked after

The Little Car and his Driver were very fond of each other. They had known each other a long time.

The Driver understood every sound that the Little Car made.

Sometimes the Little Car said 'Pink! Pink! Pink!'

'Ah!' the Driver would say. 'He wants a new gasket.' And he would fit it on, and the Little Car would be pleased.

Sometimes the Little Car said 'Pop! Pop! Pop, Pop, Pop!'

'Is the hill too steep for you?' the Driver would say, kindly. 'Never mind, we're at the top now.' And the Little Car would stop saying 'Pop!' and would run quite cheerfully again. They understood each other perfectly.

Now one day, the Little Car and his Driver were out together when the Little Car said something the Driver had never heard before. 'Knock-Knock-Knock.'

'What was that?' said the Driver. He put his head on one side and listened. The Little Car said it again. 'Knock-Knock-Knock.'

The Driver couldn't understand. He got down from his seat and walked round and round the car. He looked inside the bonnet. He poked each tyre with his finger. But he couldn't think what it was the Little Car had said.

He got back into his seat and pressed the starter again. 'Oh, knock!' said the Little Car. 'Knock-Knock-Knock.'

The Driver sat still and thought. 'I know what it is,' he said at last. 'It's the bearing. I'll have to take him to a service garage to have it put right.'

So he drove the Little Car very slowly to a garage. The Little Car didn't really like going so slowly. But his Driver wouldn't let him run fast because his inside was out of order, and he was afraid he might make it worse.

When they got to the garage a man in a white coat came and poked about in the Little Car. The Little Car felt miserable because his Driver had left him in a strange place.

But just then the man put the Little Car on a special piece of floor, and he turned a handle, and 'Wheeeee!' the Little Car went right up in the air.

'I'm flying!' cried the Little Car. 'Do look at me. I'm flying!' Then the man turned the handle again, and the Little Car came down. He was so excited, he could hardly keep still. He would have slid all over the place if the man in the white coat hadn't put a brick in front of his wheel.

After that, the Little Car didn't mind at all staying in the strange garage for two or three days, and having the man in the white coat poke him about. He used to stand there wondering when the man would make him fly again. And then just as he was beginning to think the man was never going to do it again, he would suddenly wind the handle, and 'Wheeeee!' the Little Car would go up in the air again. 'I'm flying!' he cried. 'Look, I'm an aeroplane!' It was terribly exciting.

When his Driver called to take him home again, the Little Car almost felt sorry to leave. But then he saw how happy his Driver was because his inside was better again. So he said, 'Honk, Honk! Let's have a lovely run home.' And off they went, up the hills and down again, till they got to their own little garage.

Leila Berg

19

Keep out!

When John Carr was six years old, a visitor from Japan came to see his mother. She brought with her a glove puppet, a very little monkey, as a present for John. It had a round head with two black eyes, a wide smiling mouth, sticky-out ears and a long thin tail. The glove part was made of red towelling and was only just big enough for John to put his hand inside so that the puppet could move its head and arms and come alive. John called it Tembo and soon he felt the little monkey was his friend.

Tembo went with him everywhere, even to school. John kept him in his school bag, but he didn't take him out at all for fear that some boy would snatch him, or would laugh at him for having Tembo. When things went wrong, it was a comfort just to know that Tembo was there.

One hot summer's day, John and his father and mother went for a picnic into the country. Tembo went too, in the picnic basket. They chose an interesting place with plenty of rocks to lean against, a stream and a thick wood, mostly of pine trees. After a scrumptious picnic of all the things John liked best, his mother settled against a rock

warmed by the sun and said she was going to have a quiet read. 'I think I'll have a nap,' said John's father, yawning. 'What will you do, John?'

'Explore!' said John at once. 'There's the stream and rocks to climb and the wood...'

'There's a sign, KEEP OUT, too!' said his father. 'Better not go in there. I'll come and join you soon.'

John popped Tembo in the neck of his pullover, with just his head and arms poking out — he fitted in nicely because he was so small.

20

He would be company and he would like to look at things too. Then John wandered off.

First he explored along the stream and found interesting things like pebbles, a frog and even a small fish. Then as the sun was so hot, he decided he would go just a little way into the woods. He wouldn't do any harm and there was a broken-down place in the wall so it would be easy to get in.

It was pleasantly cool under the tall trees and there was a wide open space the foresters had made in front of him, so he walked slowly down that. There were many interesting things to see: toadstools of different colours, a lot of ants, and a squirrel chattering amongst the pine cones. Once he *thought* he saw a fox slinking through the undergrowth amongst some rocks. 'Look, Tembo!' he said. 'You don't see foxes every day!'

Then he surprised a brightly coloured butterfly. It flew just ahead of him, settling occasionally on some plant. Soon it fluttered off down a faint track into the thickest part of the wood. John followed, the brambles catching his shirt sleeve and tearing a little piece out of it. 'Mum won't like that!' he thought. 'But you can't be an explorer without something happening.'

He followed the butterfly for some time. Whenever he thought he would be able to catch it and perhaps hold it in his hand for a moment, it moved away. At last it flew high in the air and disappeared.

John looked round. Where was he? How dark and gloomy it was! There seemed to be trees everywhere and they were so tall he couldn't see the top of them at all and he felt very small. 'Come on, Tembo,' he said, 'we'd better go back.' So he turned round and set out in what he thought must be the right direction. He went on and on, but there were trees everywhere and never an open space. It was very quiet except for an occasional rustling in the bushes and John tried not to hear that, for he wasn't sure what it might be.

At last he stopped and said to Tembo, 'I think we're lost, Tembo, and I don't like it. What shall we do?' Tembo said nothing but he smiled so cheerfully and looked at him so kindly that John felt less afraid.

Now he began to hurry without looking where he was going. Suddenly he caught his foot in an unseen hole, twisted his ankle painfully, and fell headlong down a steep slope over sharp rocks. As he rolled over and over, helplessly, Tembo was jerked out of his pullover and caught up in some bramble bushes . . .

John's father woke and stretched his arms and yawned. 'I'd better find John,' he said.

'Mmm?' said Mrs Carr, not looking up from her book — she had just reached a very thrilling point in the story.

Mr Carr strolled along by the stream. No John there. 'I wonder if he's gone into the wood?' he thought. 'He shouldn't, but I guess I would have when I was a boy!' So he went through the gap and walked along the open space as John had done, calling 'John! Hi, John!' every now and then. No answer!

He ran towards the tree and there, swinging in the brambles, was Tembo, smiling and waving as the wind caught his arms.

'John, John!' shouted Mr Carr again and this time there was a faint answer. When his father scrambled down the steep slope, there was John lying at the bottom, covered with scratches, his clothes muddy and torn, and his ankle so swollen that he couldn't stand on it.

'Climb on to my back and I'll give you a piggy-back,' said John's father. 'If it hadn't been for Tembo, I would never have found you!'

'I knew I'd be all right if I had Tembo,' said John, as he tucked the little puppet into his pullover again. 'Good old Tembo!'

'And next time, John,' said his father, 'KEEP OUT!'

Eileen Colwell

His eye was caught by something blue; a tiny shred of material on a bramble. 'John had been wearing a blue shirt, hadn't he? I'd better try this way,' he said to himself and he pushed his way along the narrow track. 'John!' he shouted again and again. 'Where are you, John?' But there was no answer.

It was just as he was going to turn back and try another path that he saw something bright red, just a speck against the bark of a tall pine tree. Had John had anything so bright with him? Oh, of course, Tembo!

The hot potato

Once upon a time there lived a cow whose name was Dot. She was very fond of hot potatoes. One day she swallowed one whole without chewing it, and it was so hot inside her that it hurt, and she began to cry. Great big tears rolled down her cheeks.

The farmer, whose name was Mr Smith, got a bucket to catch her tears in, so that they wouldn't make the floor all wet.

'Whatever is the matter, Dot?' he asked.

'I swallowed a hot potato,' said Dot.

'You poor thing,' said Mr Smith. 'Open your mouth.' Dot opened her mouth and smoke came out. What was to be done?

Mr Smith picked up the bucket of tears and poured it down Dot's throat. There was a sort of sizzling noise, and Dot smiled because she felt better.

That evening, when Dot was lying in her byre, eating some hay, she made up a song:

When you eat potatoes hot,
Be sure you chew them quite a lot
Or you'll get a pain inside,
Like the time I did and cried,
Because I didn't stop to chew
My potato through and through.
What a silly cow I am!
What a silly cow I am!

And that is all Dot wrote because, just then, she fell asleep.

Donald Bisset

Mrs Peck Pigeon

Mrs Peck Pigeon
   Is picking for bread;
Bob, bob, bob,
   Goes her little round head.

Tame as a pussy cat
   In the street,
Step, step, step,
   Go her little red feet.

With her little red feet
   And her little round head,
Mrs Peck Pigeon
   Goes picking for bread.

Eleanor Farjeon

The little hare and the tiger

It was ten o'clock on a sunshiny morning. The kind of morning that makes everyone happy and cheerful. But no one seemed at all happy or cheerful in the forest that day. The little hare was sitting in an open space among the bushes at the edge of the wood; he was shaking his head and saying over and over again, '*No*, I shall not go.'

'No,' said the little hare, 'I shall not go. *No*,' said the little hare, very firmly and loudly. 'I *certainly* shall not go.'

By his side sat the jackal, who was saying, 'Oh, do go. Do, *do* go. Dear hare, dear, kind, beautiful hare, *do* go.'

And each time the jackal spoke, the little hare shook his head till his ears flapped, and said, 'No, *no*, I shall *not* go.'

Some of the other animals were peeping anxiously out of the bushes. The deer was there, the buffalo, the porcupine, the fox, the pig, the peacock, and many others. They all seemed very worried. Now I will tell you what it was all about.

24

Some time before this story begins, a large and hungry tiger had to come to live in the forest. Every day he prowled about looking for food, and every day he killed two or three of the animals. He really killed many more than he needed to eat. Everyone was afraid of him, and no one could feel happy or comfortable.

But one day the jackal had a bright idea – at least it seemed bright to *him*. He called a meeting of the animals and told them of his plan. 'Suppose,' said the jackal, 'we promised to send one animal every day for the tiger's dinner. Then the rest of us would be safe that day, for he would not go roaring through the forest killing everyone he met.' (And the jackal thought in his cunning head, 'We could send all the small animals first, and then *I* should be safe for a very long time.')

The other animals agreed. The tiger agreed. He was growing fat and lazy, and it saved him trouble. Everyone was pleased, except the little hare. When they told him he was to run along and be the tiger's dinner, he was not pleased at all.

So now you know why everyone in the forest was so worried that beautiful sunshiny morning. The animals were all afraid that if the tiger was kept waiting for his dinner he might come to fetch it and perhaps fetch several of them as well.

But nobody could persuade the little hare to go, and nobody wanted to go instead of him. The sun crept up and up the sky until it was shining just overhead, which meant that it was twelve o'clock. All the little hare would say when they told him how badly he was behaving, was, 'Don't disturb me. I am thinking.' And by this time the tiger could plainly be heard roaring with rage, but luckily he was too fat and lazy to trouble to leave his den.

However, twelve o'clock in the forest is a hot and sleepy time of day. Presently the tiger was quiet; even the jackal stopped talking, and most of the animals were having a little midday nap. So they were all very much surprised when, just as the shadows of the rocks and trees had grown large enough to show that it was one o'clock, the little hare suddenly gave a jump and a shout. 'I'm off,' he said. And off he went, running so fast that it really seemed as if he would fall head over heels. And when the animals saw which way he was running they all gave a great sigh, or a squeak, or a grunt of relief, and began to look about to see what they could find for their dinners.

Where do you think the little hare was going? You will be very surprised to hear that he ran straight to the cave where the tiger lived. He was in such a hurry that when he got there it seemed as if he couldn't stop himself, and he almost tumbled into the tiger's paws. But not quite into them; he was very careful to keep just out of reach. The tiger was very angry at having been kept waiting so long, but he had been dozing and was still only half awake. So instead of putting out his big paw to catch the little hare, he growled, 'Come here, you miserable little creature, and don't tumble about like that. What do you mean by being so late?'

The little hare began to sob. 'Oh, my lord tiger,' he said, 'I am so thin, and my brother was so fat.'

'Then why didn't they send him instead?' roared the tiger.

'They did,' said the little hare; 'they did. Oh, they did. But the other tiger got him first.'

'Who-oo-oo-oo-oo?' roared the tiger.

'The other tiger,' sobbed the little hare, 'who lives in the hole among the bushes near by.'

'Take me to him,' roared the tiger. 'I will teach him to eat my dinner and leave a miserable thing like you.'

'Very well,' said the little hare, still sobbing. 'Very well. Come this way, my lord. Come quietly, and I will take you to his den.'

And the little hare led the tiger to a narrow path which wound in and out amongst the tall grass. Tigers are like cats, they cannot see very well in the bright sunlight, and the tiger blinked and peered this way and that. Suddenly the little hare darted into some bushes. 'This way, my lord,' he said, 'this way.' The tiger leaped over the bushes and landed in a little open space. There was a deep hole, by the side of which stood the little hare. 'Here is the den, my lord,' he said, in a trembling voice. 'Oh! Oh! Oh! I am so frightened. Let me stand close beside you!'

The tiger went to the edge and looked. There, looking up at him out of the hole, was the face of a very angry tiger, and beside him a very frightened hare.

'*Give me my dinner*!' roared the tiger, and he jumped – and splash! He went, down and down and down. And he never came up any more.

For the hole was a deep well, filled with water as clear and shining as a looking-glass, and the tiger with whom he was so angry was really his greedy self with the little hare at his side.

As for the little hare, he went scampering back to the open space where the story begins. And there he found a hollow log and climbed upon it, and he drummed with his strong hind legs and sang:

'Come! Come! Come!
I beat upon the drum.
Pr-r-rump, pr-r-rump, pr-r-rump,
I saw the tiger jump.
Down in the well he fell,
As I am here to tell.
Pr-r-rump, pr-r-prump, pr-r-rump.
I saw the tiger jump!'

The animals came creeping out of the bushes to listen, and when the little hare had sung it all through they all joined in and sang joyfully in chorus:

'Down in the well he fell:
The hare is here to tell.'

till they were all quite hoarse with singing. And they all went happily home to sleep.

Elizabeth Clark

Alfred and the fierce, fiery fox

Once upon a time – yesterday was it? – there was a boy called Alfred who didn't believe in things. He didn't believe in dragons, for instance, or witches, or magic lamps – he didn't believe in *anything*, Alfred didn't. He was in great danger of growing up to be impossibly dull and boring, when one day something happened to change his mind. It not only changed his mind, it changed Alfred.

Alfred lived in the town. He lived in a flat fourteen storeys up. This meant that he lived in two worlds. He lived in a high, 'I'm the king of the castle' world, where he looked down on things from way up high, like a bird or a man on long stilts. Instead of houses, he saw roofs; instead of people, he saw hats; and when the moon came up at night, he felt it was so near that he could almost touch it, or talk to it. (Not that he believed in the man in the moon, of course.)

The other world, the one he saw when he went down in the lift with his mother, was very different. Instead of looking down, he had to look up. In fact, every day of his life he found himself being surprised at how big people really were.

Each night when he lay in bed, Alfred's mother sang a song to him. And one particular night she sang a song from a picture book she had brought from the library:

The fox went out on a chilly night,
Prayed for the moon to give him light;
For he'd many a mile to go that night
Before he reached the town-o.

She sang it all the way through, and Alfred listened. He heard how the fox came to the town to hunt and how the farmer fetched his gun; but the fox stole the goose and ran back to his den, and there:

The fox and his wife without any strife
Cut up the goose with a carving knife.
They never had such a supper in their life,
And the little ones chewed on the bones-o.

'What's a fox?' Alfred asked when the song was finished. 'What's a fox *look* like?' because he liked the *sound* of the fox very much indeed. A fine, bold, splendid fellow he seemed to Alfred.

'Here,' said Alfred's mother. 'I'll show you.'

She began to sing the song again, and this time she showed him the book at the same time, turning the pages slowly one by one.

And for the first time in his whole life Alfred saw what a fox looked like. He saw a creature; fiery red and fierce, leaping across the pages with lolling tongue and greedy eye. And that fox, with his family of little foxes, hidden away in his secret den, was the most beautiful, wicked, magic thing Alfred had ever known.

'Again!' he cried when his mother had finished the song. 'Again!'

'Not now,' she said, and closed the book.

Alfred opened his mouth to scream. He found that just opening his mouth usually worked. His actual scream was very loud indeed. Ear-splitting, in fact. It worked tonight. His mother sang the song again, and

again Alfred looked at the pictures of the gay red fox leaping through the moonlight.

When it was over, he said, '*We* live in the town-o. It says in the song that the fox went to the town-o.'

'Yes, but not this town, dear,' said his mother. 'Don't worry — there are no foxes in this town.'

'There is,' said Alfred. 'There is.'

'No, dear,' said his mother. 'I promise you.'

'There is, there is, there is!' said Alfred. He wanted above all things for there to be a fierce, fiery fox hunting through the moonlight in *his* town, past his very window.

'All right, dear,' said his mother. 'There is. Now, go to sleep.'

She put out the light.

'And the little ones chewed on the bones-o,' said Alfred, lovingly. 'They must have had big *teeth*, even if they were little.'

'That's right. Good night, dear.'

And she went out, leaving the door open so that a band of light came in from the hall

and lit up Alfred's fort on the chest of drawers.

'There *is* a fox in this town-o,' said Alfred to himself.

So sure was he of this, that after a minute or two he crawled from under the tightly tucked blankets, opened the curtain, and kneeling on the bed, looked out.

The lights of the town lay below him. Then there was a band of dark, and then the

moon, on a level with Alfred himself, or so it seemed.

'The moon is over the town-o!' muttered Alfred under his breath. 'Now for the fox-o! Come quickly, fox, come quick!'

And as he stared into the pattern of familiar lights, he grew so hungry, so ravenous, for the sight of a fox with red plumy tail, that he knew he must see him that very night.

And he stared and stared so hard that when the fox *did* come, it was as if Alfred had *made* him come.

The fox was so beautiful, so fierce and fiery, and he leapt so silently out of the stars that Alfred banged his fists on the windowsill with unbearable excitement. And the fox was bigger than the fox on the pages had been; bigger, more shining russet, more marvellous in every way.

He strode through the sky with the moonlight on his back, tipping each separate hair with a cold, blinding fire. And down he stepped, always down, till he reached the roofs and chimneys of the town below. And there he hunted under Alfred's worshipping gaze. He leaped from house to house, stepping light on roofs under which people slept or talked, or watched television. And none of them knew or even dreamed that the fox was so near, snuffling and searching over their very heads. A wild, greedy, untamed fox had come to the town and was stamping it under his feet. Hither and thither he ran and bent his head and sniffed.

'The goose!' called Alfred. 'Where's the goose?'

And no sooner had he spoken than the geese were there, too. It was as if they had been made out of his words.

A gaggle of geese stormed over the rooftops. Alfred did not hear them, but he saw them go into a whirlwind, like a catherine-wheel of white wings and stiffened necks. And they too were bigger and whiter and more gloriously fat and panicky than the goose Alfred had seen in the pages of the book.

The fox stopped. Stockstill he stood on a steep roof. Then he lifted his head. The fur on his back stood stiff and separate; the moon struck sparks along it right to the tip of his brush.

Then he sprang.

'Quick, fox, quick!' called Alfred.

The geese scattered and the fox picked one, just one, and the chase was on. Fox and goose went vaulting then, mad and quick, the goose frantic and the fox bent to kill. And Alfred, drumming his fists on the windowsill, was willing them both to win, wanting the goose to go free *and* the fox to kill. But it was the fox he watched, his own fierce, fiery fox, and he knew what the end of the chase must be. Part of him wanted the

30

'Oh goose, *poor* goose!' and Alfred rubbed his eyes with his fists. But he saw the blurred red fire that was his fox leap smoothly back into the air and start his journey home, and Alfred was proud of him, and glad. The fox deserved his prize. He was back among the stars now, growing smaller every minute. Soon he would be in his den. Alfred pictured his little ones: eight, nine, ten, and could almost hear them cry:

> Daddy, better go back again
> For it must be a mighty fine town-o!

And he knew in his heart of hearts that there were as many geese left as he, Alfred, wanted there to be. That the fierce, fiery fox could have a goose every night of his life, if only he came to Alfred's town-o.

The fox was only a red spark now. Alfred let the curtain drop. He got back into bed and lay still, seeing again the blazing trail of the fox among the chimneys. He decided not to tell his mother.

'She wouldn't believe it,' he thought.

But Alfred did. For once you can make your own foxes, you have to believe in them. And there is a fox waiting to be made in every town-o. Just waiting . . .

Helen Cresswell

goose to go flapping free and hide amongst the chimney stacks and keep safe till dawn when the fox must go. But he thought of the little ones − eight, nine, ten − ten red foxes waiting supperless in their secret den among the stars.

'Get him, fox!' he shouted. 'Quick, get him!'

Because he could not bear to watch any longer, he shut his eyes, and when he opened them, the goose was dangling in the fox's mouth, and the fox was heading home.

If I were an apple

If I were an apple
And grew upon a tree,
I think I'd fall down
On a good boy like me.
I wouldn't stay there
Giving nobody joy;
I'd fall down at once
And say, 'Eat me, my boy.'

Anon

What a surprise!

Joe lives right on top of a high, high house with his father and mother and Charlie-boy the budgie, and Timothy lives right at the bottom of a high, high house with his father and mother and Alfie the cat. They are both friendly, happy boys and like their homes very much.

When the weather was bad and they couldn't go out they tried not to make too much fuss, because they knew that when they could go out again they might be lucky enough to go to the playground, and if they went to the playground they might see each other. It made so much difference now they were friends.

One day however, a nasty thing happened. Poor Joe woke up with spots all over himself and a funny feeling in his head, and the lady-doctor who climbed all the way up the stairs to see him said he had measles. Poor Joe! He had to stay indoors, even though the weather was nice, and that made him very miserable.

And would you believe it, Timothy was miserable too, because *he* had woken up with spots as well, and *his* head felt funny, and the gentleman-doctor who went to see him said he had measles, too!

I suppose they must have caught it at the same time.

When Joe got up and saw the sunshine dancing on all the roofs that were lower than theirs, he grew very bored and cross. He said, 'Oh, what will my friend Timothy think if I'm not at the playground?'

And when Timothy got up he wondered about Joe. 'I hope Joe won't forget me.'

Well now, it wasn't long before Joe felt much better, and tired of having to stay at home. He thought, 'I know! I can't go outdoors yet, but I *can* take a walk through the house. Why, that would be quite an adventure!'

Now Joe had walked down the stairs lots of times with his Mum or his Dad, but of course it isn't an adventure unless you do it on your own, is it? So, without saying a word, Joe opened the door: and there were the steep stairs going down, down, down.

So down, down, down went Joe. On every landing there was a door; and when he came to a door he remembered to walk very, very quietly, so as not to disturb anyone; but when he was on the staircase part he sang a little song that the Special Lady had taught the children to sing in the playground.

On that very same day, Joe's friend Timothy was feeling better too. He was so tired of looking out of the window and seeing people's feet going by on the pavement above his head that *he* decided to have an indoor adventure, too! He decided that it would be fun to go outside and climb all the way up through the house.

Now Timothy had never been upstairs in the house before because his family had a special under-the-pavement front door with steps up to the roadway; but there was a door at the back of his mother's bedroom that opened into the house, so he went through that.

The first thing he saw was the staircase going up, up, up. So *up* he went. It *was* a climb. Up and up.

On to a landing and softly past a door went Timothy, and as he climbed the stairs he sang too. *He* sang one of the Special Lady's songs. He sang:

'Oh, the grand old Duke of York
He had ten thousand men –
He marched them up to the top of the hill
And he marched them down again . . .'

Then Timothy stopped singing for a moment, because he was coming to a landing, but, do you know, the *song* didn't stop. It went on – like this – soft at first but getting louder and louder:

'. . . up to the top of the hill
And he marched them down again.
And when they were UP – they were UP,
And when they were DOWN –
                    they were DOWN,
And when they were only half-way up
They were neither up nor down.'

And Joe looked down, and Timothy looked up!

And there they were! They had been living in the same house all the time, and they hadn't known it. They *were* pleased to see each other!

They sat down on the stairs side by side and told each other about their measles.

Then Joe said, 'Now you will be able to visit my upstairs home, and I can visit your downstairs home. Won't that be nice?'

And that was just what did happen.

Of course, their mothers were very cross at first when they found they had gone out into the big house on their own like that, but afterwards they both said how pleased they were to see what a nice friend each little boy had made.

Now when the boys go to the park, sometimes Joe's Mum takes them, and sometimes Timothy's. Sometimes they go with both mothers together. When both mothers go they have to take it in turns to sit in their own favourite parts of the park, but of course Joe and Timothy go straight to the playground.

Dorothy Edwards

The bus that wouldn't go

One morning Red Bus woke up in a very bad temper. 'I'm tired of always having to get up so early,' he grumbled. 'I'm tired of having to go out on wet cold mornings. I'm tired of carrying people to their work. In fact I've made up my mind that I'm not going to do it any more.' So when his driver came to fetch him he just wouldn't start. He stood quite still in front of the garage door, so that none of the other buses could get out.

'Now, now,' said the driver, 'come along, old fellow. Get a move on do, or we'll be late at the first stop.'

'As if *I* cared about that!' snorted the bus and made rude noises in his inside. His driver got down from his seat and lifted the bonnet to see if he could find out what was wrong, but every time he touched anything the bus went sputter-sputter-spit back at him in a very angry manner. The poor man scratched his head and then he turned a big handle at the front. Bang! Bang! Bang! Splutter! went the bus, but he didn't move an inch.

The other buses began to get angry because they could not get out of the garage. They started blowing their horns and shouting at Red Bus to get out of the way, but he pretended not to hear them. He stood firmly in the middle of the roadway and would not budge.

Outside at the first stop all the people were waiting.

'What has happened?' they asked each other. 'Red Bus is never late. He always comes on time,' and they looked anxiously along the road.

'I'll miss my train,' said the tall man.

'I won't be able to open my shop,' said the short one.

'I won't get to my office,' said the pretty girl.

'We won't be able to get to school!' said the children.

Then they all said, 'Hurry up Red Bus – *do*.'

But the bus didn't come. He was still standing in front of the garage door.

The driver stood in the midst of all the other bus drivers talking things over, and at last one of them had a good idea.

'There's a door at the back,' he said. 'It's smaller than the front one, but Red Bus is much bigger than any of the other buses, so I think that if we took down the posts at each side they might manage to get through. We'll show old Grumpy we can do without him.'

Now when Red Bus heard that, he came out of his sulks in a hurry, and he started to make his engine run, as if he would be off at any moment.

'Bless my soul!' said his driver. 'Do you hear that?' and he leapt up on to the driver's seat and grasped the wheel just as Red Bus rolled out on to the roadway.

'Do without me indeed! I'll let them see if they do,' spluttered Red Bus, and fairly flew along the street.

When the people at the stop saw him coming, they waved and shouted, 'Good old Reddy,' they cried. 'We knew you'd turn up,' and they piled inside.

'I'll catch my train,' said the tall man.

'I'll open my shop,' said the short one.

'I'll get to my office,' said the pretty girl, and...

'We'll be in time for school,' said the children. 'Hurrah!'

Between you and me, Red Bus felt very ashamed of himself when he saw how pleased the people were to see him and how fond of him they all were.

'I can't think what was the matter with me,' he said. 'Perhaps my driver was right and I needed more oil in my inside.' At any rate I can tell you that he never, never, never was late again.

Margaret Law

Down the stream

Down the stream the swans all glide;
It's quite the cheapest way to ride.
Their legs get wet,
Their tummies wetter:
I think after all
The bus is better.

Spike Milligan

35

J for John

John was very excited for it was his birthday — and what luck, it was snowing!

He ran downstairs to breakfast, in great excitement. The table was laid for breakfast and there was a special brown egg for him. But instead of the usual pile of presents beside his plate, there was only one little box.

John felt very disappointed. Was he only going to have one present this year?

His mother smiled. 'Open that box, dear, and see what's inside it,' she said.

John opened it. Inside there were three keys — a big one, a middle-sized one and a small one. There was a piece of paper too, and on it was printed a big letter 'J'.

'What is it, Mummy?' he asked. He felt very puzzled.

'Well,' said his mother, 'Daddy and I thought that as it's not long since you had your Christmas presents, you might like to have your birthday presents in a different kind of way. We've hidden three presents for you. When you find out where these keys fit, you'll find your presents too. Each one will have a big 'J for John' tied on to it so that you will know it is yours.'

'Can I begin looking now?' asked John eagerly.

'When you've eaten your breakfast.'

Breakfast over, John had a good look at the three keys. 'I'll try the middle one first,' he decided. 'It looks the easiest.' He ran round the house in a great hurry, trying to fit the key in all kinds of locks. Some were too large so that the key almost disappeared in them, others were too small so that the key wouldn't go in at all. He had no luck downstairs, so went upstairs to his mother's room. He tried the drawer in the dressing-table and the chest of drawers and, last of all, the wardrobe. The key fitted — CLICK — it turned and he looked inside.

There were his mother's dresses and her fur coat. John rubbed his face against it —

he liked its softness. But where was his present? He rummaged about and there was a box. Tied to it was a label with a big 'J for John' on it.

He sat down on the floor to open the box. Inside was a pair of wellingtons; real boy's wellingtons. 'I'll be able to go out in the snow even when it's as deep as deep,' he thought.

Now he chose the small key. It was too small for the doors of the rooms, too big for his mother's little bureau. But one of the drawers in the sideboard was locked, and when he fitted the key in the keyhole — CLICK — it turned. Inside among the tablecloths was a parcel wrapped in gay paper, and tied on to it was a label with a big 'J for John' printed on it.

John tore open the paper. There was a special kind of woollen cap with flaps to go over his ears — just like the one his father had brought back from Canada. Now his ears would be warm in the snow.

There was only the big key left. 'Wherever does this one fit?' he asked his mother.

He opened the door. Brrr- how cold it was. The lawn was white and smooth except for the little criss-cross marks made by the birds' feet. He put his foot in the snow – it was quite deep. But his father had cleared a path to the garage and to the shed.

Big flakes of snow were falling and tickling his nose. He plodded to the shed door and put the big key in the lock. It fitted. He had to use both hands to turn it, but – CLICK – it opened the door.

Inside the shed were his father's garden tools and his lawn mower. There was the wheelbarrow, but where was his present? Suddenly he saw it – a large parcel wrapped in brown paper and on top of it was a label, 'J for John'.

'I mustn't tell you,' she said, 'but I *think* you've often seen someone using it.'

John sat down by the fire and thought. Whoever would use a big key like that? Why, his father of course! 'I know,' he shouted. 'Can I go outside in the snow and try it?'

'Wrap up warmly,' said his mother.

'I shall put on my new wellingtons,' said John busily, 'and my new cap.'

'And your coat,' said his mother.

Soon John was dressed and ready.

Whatever could be inside the parcel? It was quite long but not very tall. He tore a corner of the paper and peeped through. He could see something made of wood. Could it be? He stripped off the paper in a hurry – yes, it was a sledge, the thing he had wanted more than anything! It was a beauty too – with shining runners and a thick cord to pull it by.

What a good thing it was Saturday tomorrow and his father would have a holiday. What fun they would have!

And so they did, rushing down the hill on the sledge, falling into the snow and climbing the hill to do it all over again.

It was the most exciting birthday John had ever had.

Vera Colwell

The baker's cat

Once there was an old lady, Mrs Jones, who lived with her cat, Mog. Mrs Jones kept a baker's shop in a little tiny town at the bottom of a valley, between two mountains.

Every morning you could see Mrs Jones's light twinkle out long before all the other houses in the town, because she got up very early to bake loaves and buns and jam tarts and Welsh cakes.

First thing in the morning Mrs Jones lit a big fire. Then she made dough out of water, flour and sugar and yeast. Then she put the dough into pans and set it in front of the fire to rise.

Mog got up early too. *He* got up to catch mice. When he had chased all the mice out of the bakery, he wanted to sit in front of the warm fire. But Mrs Jones wouldn't let him, because of the loaves and buns there, rising in their pans.

She said, 'Don't sit on the buns, Mog.'

The buns were rising nicely. They were getting fine and big. That is what yeast does. It makes bread and buns and cakes swell up and get bigger and bigger.

As Mog was not allowed to sit by the fire, he went to play in the sink.

Most cats hate water, but Mog didn't. He loved it. He liked to sit by the tap, hitting the drops with his paw as they fell, and getting water all over his whiskers!

What did Mog look like? His back, and his sides, and his legs down as far as where his socks would have come to, and his face and ears and his tail were all marmalade coloured. His stomach and his waistcoat and his paws were white. And he had a white tassel at the tip of his tail, white fringes to his ears, and white whiskers. The water made his marmalade fur go almost fox colour and his waistcoat shining-white clean.

But Mrs Jones said, 'Mog, you are getting too excited. You are shaking water all over the pans of buns, just when they are getting nice and big. Run along and play outside.'

Mog was affronted. He put his ears and tail down (when cats are pleased they put their ears and tail *up*) and he went out. It was raining hard.

A rushing, rocky river ran through the middle of the town. Mog went and sat *in* the water and looked for fish. But there were no fish in that part of the river. Mog got wetter and wetter. But he didn't care. Presently he began to sneeze.

Then Mrs Jones opened the door and called, 'Mog! I have put the buns in the oven. You can come in now, and sit by the fire.'

Mog was so wet that he was shiny all over, as if he had been polished. As he sat by the fire he sneezed nine times.

Mrs Jones said, 'Oh dear, Mog, are you catching a cold?'

She dried him with a towel and gave him some warm milk with yeast in it. Yeast is good for people when they are poorly.

Then she left him sitting in front of the fire and began making jam tarts. When she had put the tarts in the oven she went out shopping, taking her umbrella.

But what do you think was happening to Mog?

The yeast was making him rise.

As he sat dozing in front of the lovely warm fire he was growing bigger and bigger.

First he grew as big as a sheep.

Then he grew as big as a donkey.

Then he grew as big as a cart-horse.

Then he grew as big as a hippopotamus.

By now he was too big for Mrs Jones's little kitchen, but he was *far* too big to get through the door. He just burst the walls.

When Mrs Jones came home, with her shopping-bag and her umbrella, she cried out, 'Mercy me, what is happening to my house?'

The whole house was bulging. It was swaying. Huge whiskers were poking out of the kitchen window. A marmalade-coloured tail came out of the door. A white paw came out of one bedroom window, and an ear with a white fringe out of the other.

'Morow?' said Mog. He was waking from his nap and trying to stretch.

Then the whole house fell down.

'Oh, Mog!' cried Mrs Jones. '*Look* what you've done.'

The people in the town were very astonished when they saw what had happened. They gave Mrs Jones the Town Hall to live in, because they were so fond of her (and her buns). But they were not so sure about Mog.

The Mayor said, 'Suppose he goes on growing and breaks our Town Hall?'

'Suppose he turns fierce? It would not be safe to have him in the town, he is too big.'

Mrs Jones said, 'Mog is a gentle cat. He would not hurt anybody.'

'We will wait and see about that,' said the Mayor. 'Suppose he sat down on someone? Suppose he was hungry? What will he eat? He had better live outside the town, up on the mountain.'

When the sheep on the mountain saw him coming, they were scared to death and galloped away. But he took no notice of them. He was looking for fish in the river. He caught lots of fish! He was having a fine time.

By now it had been raining for so long that Mog heard a loud, watery roar at the top of the valley. He saw a huge wall of water coming towards him. The river was beginning to flood, as more and more

So everybody shouted, 'Shoo! Scram! Pssst! Shoo!' and poor Mog was driven outside the town gates. It was still raining hard. Water was rushing down the mountains. Not that Mog cared.

But poor Mrs Jones was very sad. She began making a new lot of loaves and buns in the Town Hall, crying into them so much that the dough was too wet, and very salty.

Mog walked up the valley between the two mountains. By now he was bigger than an elephant – almost as big as a whale!

rain-water poured down into it, off the mountains.

Mog thought, 'If I don't stop that water, all these fine fish will be washed away.'

So he sat down, plump in the middle of the valley, and he spread himself out like a big, fat cottage loaf.

The water could not get by.

The people in the town had heard the roar of the flood-water. They were very frightened.

The Mayor shouted, 'Run up the mountains before the water gets to the town, or we shall be drowned!'

So they all rushed up the mountains, some on one side of the town, some on the other.

What did they see then?

Why, Mog sitting in the middle of the valley. Beyond him was a great lake.

'Mrs Jones,' said the Mayor, 'can you make your cat stay there till we have built a dam across the valley, to keep all that water back?'

'I will try,' said Mrs Jones. 'He mostly sits still if he is tickled under his chin.'

So for three days everybody in the town took turns tickling Mog under his chin with hay-rakes. He purred and purred and purred. His purring made big waves roll right across the lake of flood-water.

All this time the best builders were making a great dam across the valley.

People brought Mog all sorts of nice things to eat, bowls of cream and condensed milk, liver and bacon, sardines, even chocolate! But he was not very hungry. He had eaten so much fish.

On the third day they finished the dam. The town was safe.

The Mayor said, 'I see now that Mog is a gentle cat. He can live in the Town Hall with you, Mrs Jones. Here is a badge for him to wear.'

The badge was on a silver chain to go round his neck. It said, MOG SAVED OUR TOWN.

So Mrs Jones and Mog lived happily ever after in the Town Hall. If you should go to the little town of Carnmog you may see the policeman holding up the traffic while Mog walks through the streets to catch fish in the lake for breakfast. His tail waves above the houses and his whiskers rattle against the upstairs windows. But people know he will not hurt them, because he is a gentle cat.

He loves to play in the lake and sometimes he gets so wet that he sneezes. But Mrs Jones is not going to give him any more yeast.

He is quite big enough already!

Joan Aiken

Rabbits go riding

All mother Kangaroos have a pocket. One day some of the other Australian animals were jealous. 'Kangaroo has a pocket,' they said, 'why shouldn't she carry something for us!'

Up sprang Kangaroo, with long, strong leaps. And *down* came Kangaroo thumping on the ground.

'Carry my leaves in your pocket,' called Koala, and he threw them into Kangaroo's pouch.

'They prickle,' said Kangaroo, but over the spinifex grass she leapt.

'Carry my ants,' called little Echidna, and he threw them into Kangaroo's pouch.

'They tickle,' said Kangaroo, but over the yellow wattles she leapt.

'Carry my frog in your pocket,' called Snake.

'It's cold and jumpy,' said Kangaroo, but on she went between the gum trees.

'Carry my pineapple,' Possum called.

'It's hard and lumpy,' said Kangaroo, but on she went, over scrubland and plain.

Kangaroo jumped with short, tired hops, with the leaves that prickled, the ants that tickled, the jumpy frog, and the lumpy pineapple. Her pouch looked just like a shopping basket.

'Now I am home at last,' she sighed, and she lay down in the dust bath beneath her tree.

'Thank you,' the lazy creatures said. 'You can carry our things again tomorrow.'

'Oh, I'm so tired,' sighed Kangaroo. 'But they *will* keep throwing things in my pouch.'

Then she lay in the shade and tried to sleep.

A little later she opened her eyes. Two fat rabbits sat side by side. Kangaroo saw that their fur was ruffled. Their paws were sore, and their tails were dusty.

'Please, Mrs Kangaroo,' they said. 'Which is the way to the farmer's grasslands?'

Kangaroo looked towards the hills, which were blue and misty and far away.

'Between the gum trees and over the hills, at the end of a long black road,' she said.

The rabbits sat down on their dusty white tails, and stared at each other with tears in their eyes.

'Then we'll never get home tonight,' they said. 'We're tired and lost, and a little bit frightened. We want to go home. We want it so much.'

Kangaroo looked at the sad little rabbits. Then she stretched her aching legs, and said, 'Jump into my pocket. I'll carry you home.'

The fat little rabbits jumped into her pouch.

Kangaroo jumped between the gum trees. The rabbits felt soft and warm in her pouch. They wriggled and giggled and squealed with delight.

'Thump, we are down, we are down,' they said. 'Up, we are up. We are down. We are up.'

'Carry my leaves in your pocket,' called Koala, and he threw them into Kangaroo's pouch.

'Rubbish,' giggled the fat little rabbits, and they scooped up the leaves in their strong little paws, and threw them back at Koala.

Kangaroo reached the foot of the hills.

'Carry my ants,' called Echidna, and he threw them into Kangaroo's pouch.

'Tickly things!' the rabbits squealed. 'They'll get into our fur.' And they threw them away.

Kangaroo leapt to the top of the hills.

'Carry my frog in your pocket,' called Snake, and he threw it into Kangaroo's pouch.

'Full up! No room!' called the fat little rabbits, and they tossed the jumping frog into a salt bush.

Kangaroo reached the long black road.

'Carry my pineapple,' Possum called, and he threw it into Kangaroo's pouch.

'No thanks! We're not hungry,' the rabbits shouted, and the pineapple bounced as it fell on the road.

'Thump, we are down. We are up,' squeaked the rabbits. 'Thump, we are up. We are down. We are home.'

Kangaroo lay in the long cool grass. The rabbits climbed out of her pouch and said, 'We've had such a wonderful ride in your pocket. Thank you for bringing us home so quickly.'

Kangaroo smiled.

'It was easy,' she said. 'Those lazy creatures were *very* surprised. They won't make me carry their things again.'

She was right, and never, never again did her pouch look like a shopping basket. Nor was it empty every day as she leapt over spinifex grass and hill, because over its edge peeped two furry faces.

'Here we go riding again,' squeaked the rabbits. 'Thump, we are down. We are up. We are down. Thump! We are riding in Kangaroo's pocket. How lucky we are!'

Anita Hewett

A bargain for the Brambles

Mr and Mrs Bramble had six children but very little money, so when they needed new clothes it was quite a problem. Especially when it came to shoes.

In the summer the little Brambles ran barefoot, because they liked it, but in the winter everybody had to have a good strong pair of shoes to go to school in. And the shoes wore out so fast! Mrs Bramble was always taking them to Joey Thaw, the cobbler, to be mended.

One fine, frosty morning Mrs Bramble sent all the children along to the cobbler in the charge of the eldest girl, Margery. Into Margery's hand she put a purse, and in the purse there was enough money to pay for repairs to all the children's shoes.

'You will have to sit in the shop and wait till Joey Thaw has mended them,' their mother said, because none of the Brambles had more than one pair of outdoor shoes. 'And while you are away I shall turn out the sitting-room and cook the dinner.'

Margery was very proud of taking charge of her brothers and sisters, and paying Joey Thaw for mending their shoes. But the younger ones grumbled and complained that they didn't want to waste a whole morning sitting and waiting in Joey Thaw's shop, and why couldn't she take all the shoes without them?

They grumbled all the way until they came to a fashionable shoe shop a few doors before the cobbler's, and here all the little Brambles stopped and pressed their noses against the window.

'Why can't we have *new* shoes instead of always having them mended?' they said, looking at the rows of shoes waiting to be bought, inside the window.

'Because they are much too expensive, and it is cheaper for Joey Thaw to mend the old ones!' said Margery primly. She was trying to drag her brothers and sisters away when Joseph, the eldest boy, cried out: 'Look!'

He had seen a box of shoes standing outside the shop, and on the box was a label that said: 'BARGAINS!'

There were shoes of every shape and size, boys' shoes, girls' shoes, all brightly coloured and astonishingly cheap. And they looked strong and well-made too.

While they were still staring at the shoes the shopkeeper came outside the shop.

'Yes!' he said, 'You'll never see shoes like that again! Just look at them, my dears! Those are a real bargain!'

He was a funny looking little man, rather like a goblin. Margery did not like the look of him, and again she tried to make her brothers and sisters come away from the window.

But they all began to plead with her at once.

'*New* shoes, Margery! And we can each have a pair for less than it costs to go to Joey Thaw's! And we won't have to sit and wait all the morning! They'll last much longer than all those old stitches and patches!'

At last Margery gave in. She gave the shopkeeper the money and each of the Brambles was fitted for a new pair of shoes. Even Margery herself chose a beautiful pair of blue lace-ups, and it took all the money she had in the purse.

'I hope you are satisfied!' said the queer old shopkeeper, 'Because I can't give back any money on bargain shoes! Besides, I'm shutting up shop and moving away. That's why I'm selling them off cheap!'

The Brambles were more than satisfied. They rushed out of the shop and went home to tell their mother. On the way they threw all their old shoes into the duckpond, where, being full of holes, they sank at once.

Mrs Bramble was surprised to see them home so early, and all of them with new shoes which they put on at once to show her.

But she was more surprised still when Margery began slowly to turn round and round in the middle of the kitchen floor, getting faster and faster until she was spinning like a top. At the same time Henry began to bound up and down, with his feet together like a kangaroo, while Joseph stuck his legs out and did a goose-step up and down the room.

By now Jonathan was hopping like a frog, Katie was bouncing first on one foot and then on the other, while little Thomas had crossed his legs and was walking sideways like a crab, till it made you feel cross-eyed to look at him.

'Stop! *Stop!*' cried Mrs Bramble, but the children could not stop, however hard they tried, until one after another they pulled their shoes off and became themselves again.

When she realised that it was the bargain shoes that were causing all the trouble, Mrs Bramble was at her wit's end to know what to do next.

'Take them straight back to the shop and get your money back!' she told them.

'He won't take them back!' sobbed the children. 'He said he wouldn't, because they are bargains!'

'Then put your old shoes on again!' said Mrs Bramble.

'We threw them in the duckpond!' cried the children.

'Well, you can throw this lot in after them!' cried Mrs Bramble in a rage. 'You will have to stay indoors in your slippers until your father has earned enough money to buy you new shoes, and that won't be this side of Easter!'

The children went back to the duckpond in their new shoes, and it took them a long time to get there, for Margery was twirling round and round, Henry was jumping with both feet together like a kangaroo, Joseph was doing his goose-step, Jonathan was hopping like a frog, Katie was bounding first on one leg and then on the other, and little Thomas was walking sideways, like a crab.

When they got to the duckpond they tore the shoes off their feet, filled them with stones, and hurled them as far as they could into the middle of the pond.

Then they turned to go home with their feet freezing in the cold, and nothing to wear out of doors for the rest of the winter.

Suddenly little Thomas cried out: 'Look there!'

All the Brambles turned back to look at the pond, and saw an extraordinary sight.

Like a line of little brown boats their old shoes were popping up through the duckweed and sailing towards them across the pond.

One after another each pair arrived at the bank, and were eagerly rescued by the children. And each pair of shoes was quite strong again and perfectly mended, in fact, very nearly as good as new.

Mrs Bramble did not know what to make of it, but she still said she was going back to the shop to give the shopkeeper a piece of her mind. But when she got there the shop was locked up and empty. There wasn't a pair of shoes left in the window, and the bargain box had disappeared.

So had the bargain shoes that had been thrown into the duckpond.

Though the Brambles looked for them, just out of curiosity, every time they passed by on their way to school, they were never seen again.

Ursula Moray Williams

Elephant Big and Elephant Little

Elephant Big was always boasting.

'I'm bigger and better than you,' he told Elephant Little. 'I can run faster, and shoot water out of my trunk, and eat more, and...'

'No. You can't!' said Elephant Little.

Elephant Big was surprised. Elephant Big was *always* right. Then he curled up his trunk and laughed and laughed.

'What's more, I'll show you,' said Elephant Little. 'Let's have a running race, and a shooting-out-of-our-trunks race, and an eating race. We'll soon see who wins.'

'I shall, of course,' boasted Elephant Big. 'Lion shall be judge.'

'The running race first!' Lion said. 'Run two miles there and two miles back. One of you runs in the field, the other one runs in the forest. Elephant Big shall choose.'

Elephant Big thought and thought, and Elephant Little pretended to talk to himself: 'I hope he chooses to run in the field, because *I* want to run in the forest.'

When Elephant Big heard this, he thought: 'If Elephant Little wants very much to run in the forest, that means that the forest is best.' Aloud he said: 'I choose the forest.'

'Very well,' said Lion. 'One, two, three. Go!'

Elephant Little had short legs, but they ran very fast in the smooth springy grass of the field.

Elephant Big had long, strong legs, but they could not carry him quickly along through the forest. Broken branches lay in his way; thorns tore at him; tangled grass caught his feet. By the time he stumbled, tired and panting, back to the winning post, Elephant Little had run his four miles, and was standing talking to Lion.

'What ages you've been!' said Elephant Little. 'We thought you were lost.'

'Elephant Little wins,' said Lion.

Elephant Little smiled to himself.

'But I'll win the next race,' said Elephant Big. 'I can shoot water much higher than you can.'

'All right!' said Lion. 'One of you fills his trunk from the river, the other fills his trunk from the lake. Elephant Big shall choose.'

Elephant Big thought and thought, and Elephant Little pretended to talk to himself: 'I hope he chooses the river, because *I* want to fill my trunk from the lake.'

When Elephant Big heard this, he thought: 'If Elephant Little wants very much to fill his trunk from the lake, that means the lake is best.' And aloud he said: 'I choose the lake.'

'Very well!' said Lion. 'One, two, three. Go!'

Elephant Little ran to the river and filled his trunk with clear, sparkling water. His trunk was small, but he spouted the water as high as the trees.

Elephant Big ran to the lake, and filled his long, strong trunk with water. But the lake water was heavy with mud, and full of slippery, tickly fishes. When Elephant Big spouted it out, it rose only as high as a middle-sized thorn bush.

He lifted his trunk and tried harder than ever. A cold little fish slipped down his throat, and Elephant Big spluttered and choked.

'Elephant Little wins,' said Lion.

Elephant Little smiled to himself.

When Elephant Big stopped coughing, he said: 'But I'll win the next race, see if I don't. I can eat much more than you can.'

'Very well!' said Lion. 'Eat where you like and how you like.'

Elephant Big thought and thought, and Elephant Little pretended to talk to himself: 'I must eat and eat as fast as I can, and I mustn't stop; not for a minute.'

Elephant Big thought to himself: 'Then I must do exactly the same. I must eat and eat as fast as I can and I mustn't stop; not for a minute.'

'Are you ready?' asked Lion. 'One, two, three. Go!'

Elephant Big bit and swallowed, and bit and swallowed, as fast as he could, without stopping. Before very long, he began to feel full up inside.

49

Elephant Little bit and swallowed, and bit and swallowed. Then he stopped eating, and ran round a thorn bush three times. He felt perfectly well inside.

Elephant Big went on biting and swallowing, biting and swallowing, without stopping. He began to feel ever so funny inside.

Elephant Little bit and swallowed, and bit and swallowed. Then again he stopped eating, and ran round a thorn bush six times. He felt perfectly well inside.

Elephant Big bit and swallowed, and bit and swallowed, as fast as he could, without stopping once, until he felt so dreadfully ill inside that he had to sit down.

Elephant Little had just finished running round a thorn bush nine times, and he still felt perfectly well inside. When he saw Elephant Big on the ground, holding his tummy and groaning horribly, Elephant Little smiled to himself.

'Oh, I do like eating, don't you?' he said. 'I've only just started. I could eat and eat and eat and eat.'

'Oh, oh, oh!' groaned Elephant Big.

'Why, what's the matter?' asked Elephant Little. 'You look queer. Sort of green! When are you going to start eating again?'

'Not a single leaf more!' groaned Elephant Big. 'Not a blade of grass, not a twig, can I eat!'

'Elephant Little wins,' said Lion.

Elephant Big felt too ill to speak.

After that day, if Elephant Big began to boast, Elephant Little smiled and said: 'Shall we have a running race? Shall we spout water? Or shall we just eat and eat?'

Then Elephant Big would remember. Before very long, he was one of the nicest, most friendly elephants ever to take a mud bath.

Anita Hewett

50

The cupboard

I know a little cupboard,
With a teeny tiny key,
And there's a jar of Lollypops
    For me, me, me.

It has a little shelf, my dear,
As dark as dark can be,
And there's a dish of Banbury Cakes
    For me, me, me.

I have a small fat grandmamma,
With a very slippery knee,
And she's Keeper of the Cupboard,
    With the key, key, key.

And when I'm very good, my dear,
As good as good can be,
There's Banbury Cakes and Lollypops
    For me, me, me.

Walter de la Mare

The adventures of LITTLENOSE
The giant snowball

Littlenose is a boy who lived long, long ago in the Ice Age. His friend, Two-Eyes, is a small woolly mammoth. This is the story of an adventure they had together with the fierce animals which lived in the woods in those days.

Littlenose, like all boys, loved the snow, and in the days when he lived there was usually snow to be found somewhere, at all times of the year. Two-Eyes was not so fond of it. He would join Littlenose in sliding sometimes, but he objected to the way in which the snow caught in his fur and formed into icicles. Then, when he went home, Mother would be angry as the ice melted and dripped water all over the floor.

One cold winter's day, the snow lay thick and smooth over the land. Littlenose, bundled up in his winter furs, was playing one of his favourite games. He was following tracks in the snow. This could be dangerous, because Littlenose sometimes made mistakes, and had once followed what he thought was a red deer, only to find himself suddenly face to face with a sabre-toothed tiger!

Today he was following what he hoped was a moose, and as usual Two-Eyes was walking behind, pausing from time to time to shake the snow from his coat, and give disgusted little grunts through his trunk.

The tracks were clear, and led through woods, over frozen marshland and up a long hill. Here, however, he lost them. The top of the hill was bare and rocky, and the snow had drifted clear. There was just no way of telling which way the moose had gone.

With a sigh of relief, Two-Eyes shook himself once more, then began to clean his fur with his trunk. Having done this, he found a sheltered spot behind a rock and settled down for a quiet snooze.

Littlenose, meanwhile, was doing some exploring. Down the hill a little way there was a wood, and he thought there might be something interesting to see there.

But it was just an ordinary wood. Then he found the dead tree. It had been struck by lightning and stood bare and broken. The bark had come off in great pieces, and as Littlenose looked, he had a wonderful idea. There was one piece of bark which was longer than Littlenose himself, and quite broad. It wasn't very heavy, and he was able to drag it across the ground. He pulled it out from under the trees and on to the snowy hillside.

Very carefully, he sat down on the piece of bark, and nothing happened. He pushed with his hands, and it moved a little. He pushed again, and it moved a little further. With all his might, Littlenose leaned back and heaved. The bark shot forward and the next moment he was careering down the hill.

Littlenose clung hard. He had no idea how to steer, but he laughed and shouted as his sledge bounced over the snow.

At last, with a thump, he hit a grassy tussock, and went somersaulting through the air. He landed in a deep drift, and scrambled to his feet, brushing the snow out of his hair.

He was amazed to find out how far he had travelled. The wood, and the rock where he had left Two-Eyes, seemed very far away.

It was growing late, and Littlenose knew he ought to start for home, but he wanted just one more ride on his sledge. He looked up at the opposite slope. 'If I start from up *there*,' he thought, 'I'll not only go faster because it's steeper, but maybe go a good way up towards the wood, if I'm lucky,' and he began to drag the piece of bark over the snow.

He was quite out of breath when he reached the top, and stopped for a moment to get his wind back.

Suddenly he heard something. He wasn't sure what. Perhaps it was only the wind. He heard it again, but louder, and shivered with fright as he realised what it was.

A wolf!

Almost immediately, a whole pack appeared. With one accord, they threw back their heads and howled, and came trotting across the snow.

Littlenose was terrified. He looked wildly around him for Two-Eyes, but he was far away, up on the opposite hill, beyond the wood.

In a panic, Littlenose turned and threw himself full-length on his piece of bark. It shot forward, and the next moment he was hurtling down the hill with the wolf pack in pursuit.

The snow blew up his nose and down his neck, but he didn't care. He lay flat, clinging on for all he was worth, while he bumped and rocked over the hummocky snow.

He glanced back over his shoulder.

The wolves were streaming down the hill, ears back and long red tongues hanging out. Occasionally, one would give a blood-curdling howl, and take an enormous leap forward.

However, the snow was deep for running, and Littlenose drew slowly ahead. He was almost at the foot of the hill now, and he wondered how far up the opposite side his speed would carry him. He wondered if Two-Eyes would see him from beyond the wood. He craned his neck and tried to see the little mammoth, and was so busy doing this that he didn't see a large rock straight ahead.

The sledge hit the rock with a crash, throwing Littlenose head over heels, and splintering into a thousand pieces of bark.

Littlenose, unhurt, rolled over and over. The wolves, with joyful howls, ran even faster at the thought of a boy for supper.

Littlenose scrambled up. The wolves were

almost on him, and he was a long way from the top. He began running towards an enormous, fallen pine tree. With the pack at his heels, he snatched up a thick tree branch and pulled himself up on to the roots of the fallen tree.

He was not a moment too soon.

The leading wolf sprang up with snapping jaws, and Littlenose brought the branch down hard on its nose. Yelping, it dropped back, but another came, and then another, until Littlenose was slashing and swiping as hard as he could.

He swung his branch once more, and was almost dragged down as a wolf seized it in his jaws and snatched it from him.

Now he had nothing.

But there was a lot of snow lying on the tree-trunk, and Littlenose quickly made a snowball and threw it hard. It caught a wolf in the open jaws, sending it coughing and choking away.

He threw more and more snowballs until he had almost used up all the snow.

Then the wolves drew back. Most of them had sore heads or bloody noses, and they held a council of war to decide what should be done next.

High on the hill, Two-Eyes had wakened from his nap. His fur was dry, and he felt rather hungry. It must be time to go home. He looked around him for Littlenose.

Then he heard the commotion from the foot of the hill. He couldn't see, but it sounded as if Littlenose was up to something. Having got his fur clean, he wasn't very anxious to venture on to the snowy hillside, but he carefully picked his way down to the wood.

The noise was much further on, and Two-Eyes pushed his way through the wood. The moment he saw Littlenose surrounded by the wolves, he forgot all about the snow and his fur.

He put down his head and *charged*!

But he had only taken a few paces before he realized that the slope was steeper than he had thought. He was running much too fast, and before he could stop himself he lost his footing and tumbled over and over.

Meanwhile, the wolves had decided to have one more attempt at catching Littlenose. The leader gave a howl, and the whole pack leapt forward. They were met by Littlenose's few remaining snowballs, and were almost upon him when suddenly they stopped.

They were all looking up the hill, although Littlenose couldn't see anything for the branches of the tree. Then one wolf gave a yelp and turned and ran with its tail between its legs. The rest followed and Littlenose saw why. An enormous snowball was bounding down the hill! Littlenose had never seen anything like it, and neither had the wolves. They fled madly before it, but not before several had been bowled over, and sent flying through the air.

The snowball hurtled on, and the wolves, scrambling over each other in panic, dashed madly away until their howling died in the distance. The snowball rolled a few more yards, then hit a birch sapling and burst apart in a great shower of snow.

Sitting in the middle was Two-Eyes.

'Two-Eyes,' shouted Littlenose, 'how clever of you! You arrived just in time.'

But Two-Eyes wasn't feeling particularly clever. He was so dizzy he could hardly stand. Littlenose took his trunk in one hand, and with Two-Eyes leaving a very wiggly line of footprints in the snow, they set off for home.

John Grant

56

If you find a little feather

If you find a little feather,
a little white feather,
a soft and tickly feather,
    it's for you.

A feather is a letter
from a bird,
and it says,
"Think of me.
Do not forget me.
Remember me always.
Remember me for ever.
Or remember me
at least
until
the little feather
is
lost."

So . . .
. . . if you find a little feather,
a little white feather,
a soft and tickly feather,
    it's for you.
    Pick it up
       and . . .
          put it in your pocket!

Beatrice Schenk de Regniers

Tails

Cows' tails go swishing about,
Cats' tails are twirly,
Wasps' tails have very sharp stings,
Lambs' tails are nice little things,
And pigs' tails are curly.

Anon